FOSSIL FINDER

Written by Lou Kuenzler

Illustrated by Stephen Lee

Mary Anning was born in 1799.

Her family were very poor.
They didn't have much to eat.

Mary's father showed Mary and her brother how to find pretty seashells.

They could sell them to buy a little food.

Come and buy my treasures!

When Mary's father died, the family needed the extra money more than ever.

The lady explained that fossils are the shapes plants and creatures left in the mud, long ago, after they'd rotted away.

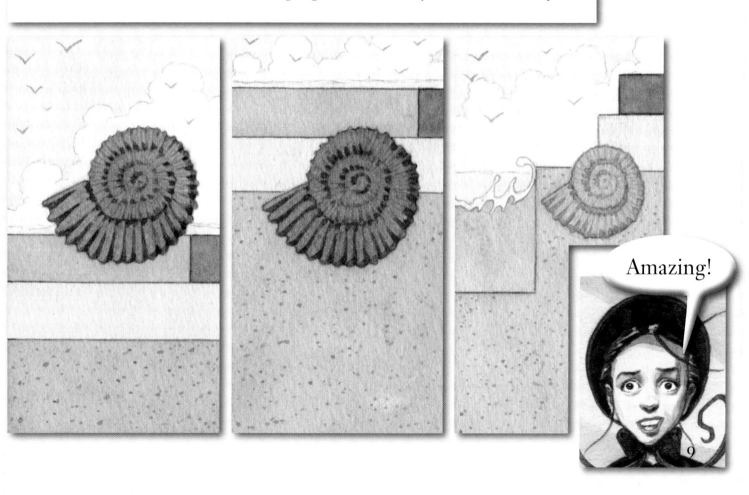

Amazing!

One day, something happened that changed Mary and Joey's lives.

Look! A shape in the rocks.

It's a fossil skull.

11

Every day, Mary chipped
away with her hammer.

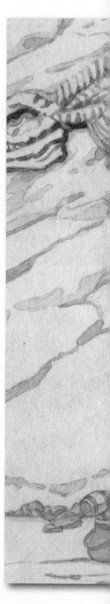

At night, she dreamt of fossils.

With one last chip, the skeleton was uncovered.

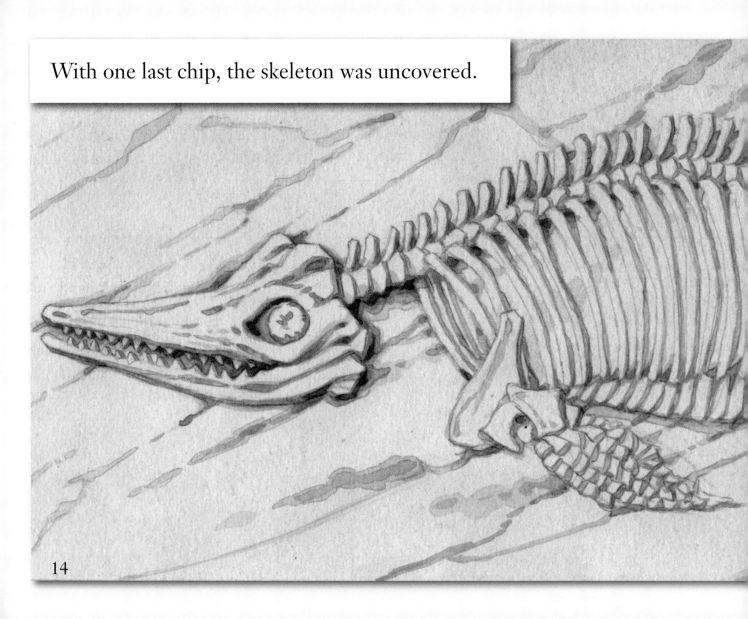

Scientists came to see the fossil.

16

Mary went on to find many more important fossils.

She helped scientists to understand ancient creatures as old as dinosaurs!

Mary never did get rich. But the fossils meant more to her than gold.

Come and see my treasures, everyone!

Science discovery report

Mary's fossil find

- Mary and her brother Joey look for fossils on the beach.

- They found a huge fossil skeleton. It was the first complete fossil of its kind.

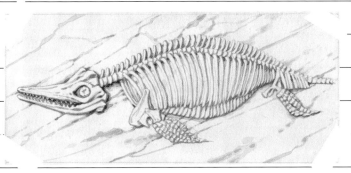

- It was a sort of fish-lizard that died out thousands of years ago.

- I bought the fossil and put it in my museum.

- This fossil will help scientists to understand ancient creatures as old as dinosaurs.

23

Ideas for reading

Written by Gillian Howell
Primary Literacy Consultant

Learning objectives: *(reading objectives correspond with Orange band; all other objectives correspond with Copper band)* read independently and with increasing fluency longer and less familiar texts; identify how different texts are organised; identify features that writers use to provoke readers' reactions; use some drama strategies to explore stories or issues

Curriculum links: Geography, History

Interest words: fossil, seashells, treasures, special, shillings, creatures, enormous, crocodiles, skeleton, monster, scientists, incredible, discovery, museum, dinosaurs

Resources: whiteboard, pens, paper, ICT

Word count: 294

Getting started

- Read the title and blurb with the children and discuss the cover illustration. Ask the children when they think this book is set and why they think this. What do they think the special thing might be? Make notes on the whiteboard.

- Ask the children to flick briefly through the pages and look at the illustrations. Explain that this is a graphic novel and an important part of what happens can be read through the illustrations. Point out the speech bubbles and remind the children to read them as they are also important to the story.

Reading and responding

- Turn to p2 and read the opening sentence together. Ask the children if they think this story is fiction or about a real person and give a reason.

- Ask the children to read the rest of the book quietly to themselves. Listen in and prompt as necessary, e.g. if they struggle with *seashells* on p3, ask them to look for two smaller words within the word to help them read it.

- Encourage the children to read the speech bubbles using an expressive tone, responding to question marks and exclamation marks.